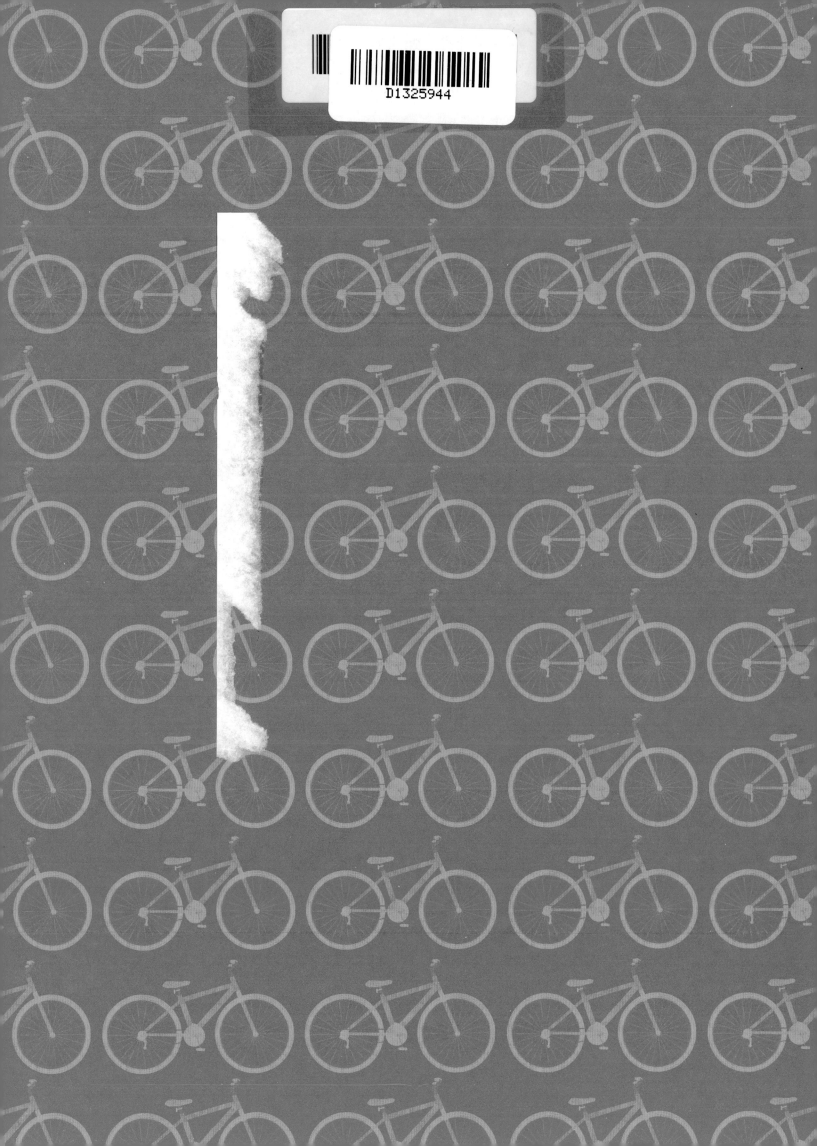

The Red Bicycle

To my family's cycling buddies, the Moreau-Nakazawa family.
Remember, when lost, listen for the distant sound of a barking dog. — J.I.

To my friend Amie, whose bicycling adventures continue to inspire people everywhere — S.S.

This edition published in 2015
by Franklin Watts
338 Euston Road
London NW1 3BH

Franklin Watts Australia
Level 17/207 Kent Street
Sydney, NSW 2000

Text © 2015 Jude Isabella
Illustrations © 2015 Simone Shin

Published by permission of Kids Can Press Ltd,
Toronto, Canada.

Edited by Valerie Wyatt

Designed by Marie Bartholomew

A CIP catalogue record for this book
is available from the British Library.

ISBN 978 1 4451 4244 9

FSC
www.fsc.org
MIX
Paper from
responsible sources
FSC® C012700

Manufactured in Malaysia in 11/2014 by Tien Wah Press (Pte.) Ltd.

Franklin Watts is a division of
Hachette Children's Books,
an Hachette UK company.
www.hachette.co.uk

The Red Bicycle

The Extraordinary Story of One Ordinary Bicycle

Written by **Jude Isabella**

Illustrated by **Simone Shin**

FRANKLIN WATTS

LONDON•SYDNEY

Leo wipes the sweat off his forehead. It's a hot day, and he's almost finished mowing the neighbour's lawn. Today he will meet his goal. He will have earned enough money to buy a new bicycle.

For two years, Leo has watched his money grow. Each time a neighbour paid him for mowing a lawn, raking leaves or shovelling snow, he would take his money to the bank. Then he would stop at the bike shop across the street to visit "his" bicycle. It has 18 gears and a suspension fork and is painted bright red.

Leo finishes mowing and collects his wages, then runs to the bank. There he withdraws the money for his bicycle. He hurries to the bike shop and watches while the owner counts the money. "Congratulations, Leo," she says. She knows how much he has wanted this bicycle.

Leo names the bicycle Big Red. He rides Big Red to school. He rides it to the swimming pool. He rides it to football practice. Leo rides Big Red everywhere.

Leo rides **Big Red** everywhere.

Leo is getting older and he's growing. One summer he grows so tall
that his knees hit Big Red's handlebars. It is time for a new bicycle.
But Leo loves Big Red. Even though the bicycle is a few years old,
he has taken good care of it, and Big Red looks almost brand-new.

He wheels Big Red into the garage, feeling a bit sad. He walks
to school thinking about what to do with the bike.

Leo wants to give Big Red to someone who will love the bicycle as
much as he does. But everyone he knows already owns a bike.

Leo wants to give **Big Red** to someone who
will love the bicycle as much as he does.

After school, Leo walks to the bike shop. The owner asks where Big Red is, and Leo explains that he has outgrown the bicycle. He needs a bigger bike, he says, and a new home for Big Red. "I have an idea for you," she says, pointing to a poster.

An organisation in town is collecting bicycles. They send the bikes to a faraway country to people who can't afford a bicycle but need one for transport. Straight away, Leo decides to donate Big Red. It will have a new home where it's really needed.

Leo wants Big Red to look its best for its trip. He washes the frame until it gleams. He oils the chain. He puts on new handgrips. His father takes a photo of Leo working on Big Red.

When he's finished, Leo hops on the too-small bicycle and rides to the shipping container where Big Red will start its new journey. This is the pair's last ride together.

The shipping container is surrounded by bikes and by people there to help out. One man demonstrates how to take apart a bicycle for packing.

Leo gets to work. He grabs a bike and unfastens the front brake. Then he removes the front tyre and pedals. He loosens the handlebars and lowers the seat. With the man's help, he ties the front wheel to the frame and the pedals under the seat.

Leo works on so many bikes he loses count. Finally, only one bicycle remains — Big Red. Leo takes apart his bicycle. He places it in the container. It is one of 462 bikes, spare parts, tools, rucksacks and footballs on the way to Africa. Leo feels a lump in his throat as the door closes.

The driver hops into
the cab and beeps the horn,
and everyone claps and cheers. Leo
waves as the truck pulls away. Goodbye,
Big Red. Have a great adventure.

At the shipping port, a crane loads the
container onto a big freighter. The red
bicycle is squeezed against the container
door. It is secure – for now. But the ocean
waves can be rough, especially in a storm.

The ship leaves port and heads south.
Containers shift around as the wind whips up
and the waves get higher. Near South America,
the ship turns and heads straight across the
Atlantic Ocean towards West Africa, hugging
the coast until it reaches Ghana.

Burkina Faso

Ghana

Goodbye, **Big Red**. Have a great adventure.

After 29 days, the red bicycle reaches land. A crane picks up the container and loads it onto a lorry. As the lorry lumbers north, the container rocks back and forth on the rough road. Big Red bangs against the door each time the lorry dips into a pothole and then out again.

Finally, the lorry stops at the city of Koudougou in Burkina Faso. But Big Red's journey is not over.

The bicycles are unloaded and reassembled. Their frames glint in the African sun. An organisation that helps widows and orphans will distribute the bicycles to families who need them. Bicycles save time and effort. Children ride them to school, and older people use them to transport goods to market.

Awa Sawadogo is a grandmother who is raising three of her grandchildren. She and her granddaughter Alisetta are waiting for a bicycle.

Alisetta gazes at the bicycles. She spots a green bike with knobby tyres and wide, upright handlebars. It looks too big. Her eyes flit from bicycle to bicycle until she sees a bright-red frame. Perfect. She can see herself breezing to market on the red bicycle.

hoping no one else will wheel it away.

One by one the new owners claim their bicycles. Alisetta locks her eyes on Big Red, hoping no one else will wheel it away. Finally, her grandmother's name is called. Only a few bicycles remain. Big Red leans against the container. Alisetta rushes over to it. "This one!" she says.

In the bush taxi on the way back to their village, Alisetta worries. She has never ridden a bicycle. Her grandmother pats her hand. "It will be no problem for you, Alisetta."

13

Alisetta leans Big Red against a baobab tree in the centre of her village. A few kids gather and then more, until it seems as if the whole village is watching. She grips the handlebars tightly. The handgrips feel nice — they're smooth and new. She hitches up her *pagne* and climbs onto the bicycle. She keeps one hand on the tree. Big Red wobbles. Alisetta hops off the seat and plants her flip-flops firmly on the ground.

Still straddling the bike, she begins to walk. Her friends clap and call out her name. Her friend Samira offers to push her. Alisetta climbs up onto Big Red, and they are off! Samira jogs alongside Big Red, holding onto its seat. Then she takes her hand away. The bicycle slows down, wobbles — and Alisetta tumbles off.

"You need to go faster," Samira says. This time when Samira lets go, Alisetta pedals hard. The bike is better behaved now.

Alisetta leaves Samira behind and pedals so fast she is soon past the last house in the village. She has done it! She stops and turns, sailing back into the village and riding circles around the cheering kids.

Awa comes to watch. She cheers along with the kids and claps to Alisetta as she sweeps by on the red bicycle.

Alisetta climbs up onto

Big Red, and they are off!

15

Over the next few weeks, Awa and Alisetta put Big Red to work.

They have a plot of land where they grow sorghum. It is ready to harvest, but there is one big problem. The birds often get to the sorghum before them. With Big Red, Alisetta can ride to the field early every morning to scare off the birds. Thanks to Big Red, they harvest more sorghum than usual.

With more sorghum, the family eats better. Awa can also make a popular drink from sorghum called *dolo*. Making *dolo* produces extra yeast and *draff*, which is good animal feed. Awa trades the *draff* with her neighbours who have livestock in exchange for more sorghum.

Alisetta begins to ride Big Red to village markets. She now has a basket to carry items for sale. She sells the extra yeast, shea butter that she and Awa make and bags she crochets out of plastic.

With the extra money, Awa sends Alisetta's younger brother and sister to school.

Over time, Big Red becomes an important part of the family. Alisetta rides to the sorghum field and the market and sometimes even gives her siblings a lift to school. Big Red is well used — and well worn.

One day, Awa takes a folded paper from her *pagne* and hands it to her granddaughter. Inside the paper is some money. Awa explains that she has been saving for another bicycle. "With two bicycles, we can earn even more," she explains.

The next day, Alisetta takes a bush taxi to Koudougou. She walks through the streets, looking at bikes for sale. She stops at a shop where a mechanic is fitting pedals onto a bright-green bicycle. It has a wire basket attached to the front. It looks the right size. She clears her throat. The mechanic looks up and smiles. "Looking for a bicycle?" he asks. Alisetta nods and points to the bike. "Yes. This one."

When Alisetta arrives back in her village with the new bicycle, she is in for a surprise. A pig has run away from its owner and ploughed through her family's courtyard, knocking into Big Red and trampling the spokes. Alisetta knows what will happen now. There is no money to fix the bicycle, so she will have to sell its parts one by one.

The new green bike will take its place, but Alisetta will miss Big Red. It was her first bicycle.

Alisetta is at the market arranging her goods when
a little pickup truck parks nearby. A man gets out. He
chats with people, eventually stopping in front of Alisetta.
His name is Boukary, he says, and he is looking for bicycles.
He works at a medical clinic that sends health workers on
bicycles to visit sick people in villages without doctors or
nurses. He needs more bikes.

Alisetta thinks about Big Red and its broken spokes.
She tells Boukary she has a bicycle, but it needs repairs.
She agrees to meet him at her house later.

When Boukary arrives, he sees a faded red bicycle
propped against a shed. He examines every bit of it: the
tyres, the wheel and its broken spokes, the frame,
the chain, the gears, the seat, the handgrips.

He nods. "We can fix it. It is a strong bicycle. We will
make it into an ambulance for the clinic."

Awa and Alisetta tell him the story of how they got
Big Red and how important it has been for the family.
Alisetta wheels Big Red to the pickup truck, pats the
seat and whispers "Thank you."

Alisetta wheels Big Red to the pickup truck

and whispers "Thank you."

Boukary takes Big Red and the other bicycles to a workshop on the outskirts of Koudougou. He sorts the bikes into two groups. Some are strong but need repairs. The others are at the end of their working lives. Boukary will use parts from them to fix the good bicycles.

Boukary's eyes fall on the faded red bicycle. Big Red looks pretty good compared to the other bikes. It has been well taken care of, but it needs stronger wheels, a new seat, new brakes and handgrips, and a paint job.

He picks up a wrench and gets to work. After a few hours of tinkering, he is done. Big Red looks almost new. Now, Boukary thinks, let's turn you into an ambulance.

With a metal hoop and nail, Boukary attaches a trailer to the bicycle. The trailer has the same tough wheels as the bicycle. On the trailer is a stretcher, propped up so a person can see out. A safety belt keeps patients safe during the ride. There is also a canopy to keep off the sun and rain. Big Red is ready for work.

Big Red is ready for work.

Haridata makes her first visit to a village on the new bicycle ambulance.

The sun is coming up, and Haridata winds a colourful scarf around her head, slips on her flip-flops and walks across the courtyard. Her mother is already pounding grain. Haridata smiles, waves and calls, "See you later." The young woman is off to the health clinic where she volunteers.

Haridata strides down the road. She wants to be on time. Today she will make her first visit to a village on the new bicycle ambulance.

A fine red dust coats everything. When she arrives at the clinic, she pauses to brush off the dust from the red bicycle ambulance parked out front.

Inside the clinic an older man is loading bandages and medicines into a medical bag.

He shakes Haridata's hand. "How are you? How is your family? What's new?"

Haridata loads the medical bag onto the back of the bicycle. She adds some bottled water and a blanket.

As she pedals to the village, she sees other bicycles pass by. One is carrying a load of something so big Haridata can barely see the rider. Another has three children clinging to it. And one has a little goat tucked into a basket on the back.

After riding for half an hour, Haridata arrives at the village. She hears the chatter of voices before she sees a crowd of people. She jumps off the bicycle, leans it against a tree and wriggles her way through the crowd.

A young boy lies on the ground, his head on a woman's lap. His eyes are scrunched shut, and he's very quiet. The woman speaks softly to the boy, patting his head. No one wants to move him. He's in pain, and his leg is lying at an awkward angle. It is broken.

Haridata speaks up. She explains who she is and points to the bicycle ambulance. Two men help her remove the portable stretcher. Haridata grabs a water bottle and some medicine to relieve the pain. The men ease the boy onto the stretcher. He cries out as they lift him. She explains that she will take him to the clinic, where a doctor can fix his leg. He must be brave, she tells him. Off they go on Big Red. At the clinic, a doctor sets the boy's leg. Haridata pats Big Red's seat as she leaves. "Good work," she says quietly.

Haridata pats **Big Red**'s seat as she leaves. "**Good work**," she says quietly.

27

Haridata's first day with the bicycle ambulance becomes a legend in the villages around the clinic. Everyone knows who she is when she rolls into town. The kids call the bike Le Grand Rouge.

Boukary regularly visits to check on the bicycle. He brings parts and keeps Le Grand Rouge working well. He's pleased the bike has a name and has done so much good.

Over the next few years, Haridata visits many villages, sometimes a three-hour ride away. The bicycle allows her to deliver medicines and bring sick people to the hospital.

One day, it's time for Haridata to move on. She has gained valuable experience with the medical clinic and Le Grand Rouge. She finds a job in a town with a bigger clinic. At the end of her last ride, she puts the bicycle away, pats the seat and whispers "Thank you."

She stares at the red bicycle for a minute, wondering where its journey began. Far away definitely, she thinks. But there is no hint that a girl pedalled along dirt roads carting goods to market or that a boy once whizzed around a small North American town on the red bicycle. But they remember Big Red, and Haridata will, too.

"Thank you, Le Grand Rouge."

What You Can Do to Help

Bicycles are fun to ride, provide great exercise and are an environmentally friendly way to get around. But in Burkina Faso and other parts of Africa and Asia, bicycles might be the only alternative to walking. People living in rural areas often find cars and fuel too expensive, and the rough, narrow roads are better suited to bicycles or motorcycles.

Bicycles can make a big difference in people's lives. They allow families to transport goods to markets, which helps them make money. The money pays for school fees, books, supplies and uniforms. With more education, children can find work when they grow up. And bicycles used as ambulances improve health care in communities. One bicycle can transform the lives of many.

How can you help? A number of organisations in the United Kingdom either collect bicycles or raise money for programmes that help people who need a bicycle but can't afford one. Some are listed here. You can find others by typing "bicycle donation, [your town or city]" into an Internet search engine. Or check for information at your local bike shop. Cyclists like to help one another! Here are some organisations to get you started:

• Re-Cycle is a non-profit organisation based in Colchester, UK. They send donated bicycles to many African countries. They work with community groups and shops to collect bicycles from all over the UK. Visit their website to find your nearest collection point. www.re-cycle.org

• World Bicycle Relief has offices in several countries around the world. It raises money to deliver strong, durable bicycles designed for people in Africa to transport heavy loads across different terrains. The bikes go to small-business people so they can transport more goods, to healthcare workers and to students. World Bicycle Relief also trains bicycle mechanics. www.worldbicyclerelief.org

PHOTO: ORRLING

A boy distributes bread near Lake Tanganyika

PHOTO: ANDREW DRESSEL

A bicycle carries a towering load of wood in Tanzania

• bikes 4 Africa delivered its first consignment of bikes to The Gambia in 2006. Its aim is to improve lives through education and has so far delivered 13,000 bikes to schools in Africa. They also donate tools and provide training to help service and maintain the donated bicycles. www.jolerider.org/programmes/bikes4africa

• The United Nations Children's Fund (UNICEF) programme Inspired Gifts will send a bicycle where it's needed for just under £70. Hold a bike-a-thon to raise money and get your friends, family, and other people in your community involved. http://shop.unicef.org.uk/Shop/p-84-Bicycle-for-a-schoolchild-or-health-worker.html

• Bikes don't have to go all the way around the world to help someone out. The Bike Station is a Scottish-based organisation that works to promote cycling in local communities. They also find ways to help communities recycle, reuse and repair bicycles for people who need one. www.thebikestation.org.uk

Instead of rusting away in a garage or shed, an unused bicycle can have a new life and create a new adventure for a boy or girl who normally would only dream about flying down the village street. A recycled bicycle can change a person's life, just as Big Red did.

About Burkina Faso

Burkina Faso, where this book takes place, means "land of honest people". This West African country is about the same size as New Zealand but, with a population of about 15 million, Burkina Faso has almost three times as many people. The people are called Burkinabé, and most live in one of the country's 8000 rural villages, without paved roads, electricity or Internet access.

Burkina Faso is landlocked – it doesn't have access to the ocean. Shipping containers with bicycles are dropped off in Ghana, a country on Burkina Faso's southern border. From there, lorries haul the containers north. Because of the high shipping costs, Burkina Faso receives fewer bicycles than other countries in Africa.

Burkina Faso is a wonderful country with a rich cultural heritage, friendly people and a diverse landscape. Find out more about the people and the country at your local library or on the Internet.

PHOTO: MICHAL SALABAN

Two men transport bananas in Uganda

A Note for Parents and Teachers

To get children involved, use **The Red Bicycle** as a centerpiece of a bicycle event. Think of the book as a hub with spokes that link to all aspects of the curriculum – writing, visual arts, technology and PSHE.

Ride and Write
In this book, Leo rides Big Red everywhere. Ask children to write about their best bicycle rides or to create an imaginary bike adventure. Ask them to develop a story or comic book starring their bikes.

Design a Bike
Look at the photographs on pages 30 and 31. Chickens are commonly transported by bicycle in many parts of the world. How would your students carry a dozen chickens, or even a goat, on a bicycle? Ask them to design a chicken or goat carrier. Take into consideration the weight and size of the animals and the fact that they won't sit still! How would children immobilise the animals so that no one—the cyclist or the animals—gets hurt?

Find a Bike a Home
Big Red ends up in Burkina Faso, West Africa. Where in the world would your children like to donate a bicycle? Ask them to research a country and make a case for why donating bikes there would be a good idea.

I'll Take My Bike
Ask children to research and list reasons why bikes are a good form of transportation in their own community. (Reasons might include that bikes are relatively cheap to buy and maintain, are pollution-free and healthy, create no parking issues and reduce road wear.)

The Bike Challenge
Bikes = health. Enlist children who have bikes to ride them more. The payoff? Perhaps they get a star on their helmets for every hour of riding. Or challenge them to ask the adults they know to sponsor them for an ongoing bike-a-thon, in which they raise money for each kilometre or mile ridden. Money raised can go towards one of the organisations listed on pages 30–31.

Bicycle Campaigns
Many towns and cities have a committee dedicated to cycling issues. Invite local cycling supporters to visit the classroom and explain what a safe bicycle infrastructure is—dedicated bicycle lanes, buses with bike racks, signage, bike parking, even bike lifts up steep hills. Have children create their own bicycle infrastructures in an imaginary town.